Attacked!

Apparently the alien didn't like Sally's tone. It took a step forward and grabbed her right arm. She shook it off—the alien didn't appear to be that strong—but it immediately grabbed her again. It pointed its weapon directly between her eyes. Sally recoiled in terror. That was enough for Adam. He was through talking. No more Mr. Nice Human.

Adam launched himself at the alien.

The alien spun on him. Leveled its weapon.

Adam saw a flash of green light. Heard Sally scream.

Then everything went black.

Books by Christopher Pike

Spooksville #1: The Secret Path
Spooksville #2: The Howling Ghost
Spooksville #3: The Haunted Cave
Spooksville #4: Aliens in the Sky

Available from MINSTREL Books

For orders other than by individual consumers, Minstrel Books grants a discount on the purchase of **10 or more** copies of single titles for special markets or premium use. For further details, please write to the Vice-President of Special Markets, Pocket Books, 1230 Avenue of the Americas, New York, NY 10020.

For information on how individual consumers can place orders, please write to Mail Order Department, Paramount Publishing, 200 Old Tappan Road, Old Tappan, NJ 07675.

CHRISTOPHER PIKE

SPOOKSVILLE™ #4

ALIENS IN THE SKY

Published by POCKET BOOKS
New York London Toronto Sydney Tokyo Singapore

This book is a work of fiction. Names, characters, places and incidents are products of the author's imagination or are used fictitiously. Any resemblance to actual events or locales or persons, living or dead, is entirely coincidental.

A MINSTREL PAPERBACK *Original*

A Minstrel Book published by
POCKET BOOKS, a division of Simon & Schuster Inc.
1230 Avenue of the Americas, New York, NY 10020

ISBN: 0-671-53728-8

First Minstrel Books printing January 1996

10 9 8 7 6 5 4 3 2 1

Front cover illustration by Lee MacLeod

Printed in the U.S.A.

Spooksville seldom got really hot. Nestled among the hills beside the ocean, Spooksville was usually cooled by a breeze preventing it from becoming uncomfortable, even in the middle of summer. But in the last half of July, only a couple of weeks after Adam Freeman and his friends got trapped in the Haunted Cave, the temperature rose sharply. At midday the thermometer burst past a hundred degrees. To get away from the heat, Sally Wilcox suggested they head up to the reservoir.

"We won't go in the water," she said. "You don't want to do that. But it's always cooler up there."

The four of them: Sally, Adam, Watch, and Cindy were seated on Cindy Makey's porch, drinking sodas and wiping their sweat-soaked foreheads. Adam stared at the half-burnt-down lighthouse—less than a quarter of a mile away—where he had wrestled with a ghost earlier in the summer. He felt as if he were about to catch fire. He couldn't remember it ever being so hot where he used to live in Kansas City, which was known for its hot summers. He wondered what had brought the heat.

"Why can't we go in the water?" Cindy asked.

"Because you'll die," Sally said simply.

"There are no fish in the reservoir," Watch added. "So there's got to be something unhealthy about the water."

"But Spooksville gets its water from the reservoir," Adam said.

"That's why so many children in this town are born mutated," Sally said.

Cindy smiled. "You were born here, Sally. That explains a lot."

"Not all mutations are bad," Sally replied.

"The water is filtered before we drink it," Watch said.

"What's filtered out?" Adam asked.

"I don't know," Watch said. "But it must be

toxic stuff. The filtration plant has a habit of blowing up every couple of years."

"Why's it cooler at the reservoir?" Adam asked.

Sally spoke. "Because Madeline Templeton—the witch who founded this city two hundred years ago—tortured fifty innocent people to death up there. The horror of that event psychically reverberates to this day, making the whole area cold as ice."

Cindy made a face. "And you want to go up there to cool off?"

Sally shrugged. "There is horror on almost every street in Spooksville, if you look deeply enough into the past. On this exact spot, where your house was built, Madeline Templeton once cut off a kid's head and fastened it onto a goat."

"Yuck!" Cindy said. "That's gross."

"Yeah, but the kid was supposed to look like a goat anyway," Watch said.

"Yeah," Sally agreed. "Maybe the witch did him a favor."

"I don't know if she tortured the people at the reservoir to death," Watch continued. "I heard she just made them go swimming in the water, and their skin turned gray and their hair fell out."

"I would rather die than lose my beautiful hair," Sally said, brushing her brunette locks aside.

"I think the area is cooler because of all the subterranean streams," Watch said, finally answering Adam's question. "If you put your ear to the ground, you definitely hear gurgling water."

Adam wiped away more sweat. "Well, should we go up there?"

Cindy was doubtful. "The Haunted Cave is up there."

"The Haunted Cave can't hurt you unless you're stupid enough to go inside it," Sally said.

"Thank you, Sally, for reminding me of my past mistake," Cindy said.

Sally spoke sweetly. "Don't mention it, Cindy."

"The Haunted Cave is high above the reservoir," Watch said. "We can't ride our bikes up that far, but we can take them as far as the reservoir. We could be there in less than twenty minutes." He tugged at his T-shirt, trying to cool off. "I wouldn't mind hanging out up there till it gets dark."

"What do you think is causing this heat?" Adam asked.

"Could be an inversion layer," Watch said.

"Or a curse from Ann Templeton," Sally said. "Madeline Templeton's seductive and evil descendant. She likes the heat. She likes all us kids to suffer in it."

Adam shrugged. "I'm for going," he said, glancing at Cindy, "if it's all right with you."

Sally leaned over and spoke in a *loud* whisper in Watch's ear. "Notice how our dear Adam doesn't make a move without checking with his sweet Cindy."

Cindy glared at Sally. "He's just being polite. That's spelled P . . . O . . . L . . . I . . . T . . . E. Look it up in the dictionary and check the meaning. I know you've never heard of the word." Cindy spoke to Adam. "My mother doesn't care what I do, as long as I'm home before dark."

"My mother doesn't care what I do as long as I don't die," Sally muttered.

Adam stood. "Then it's decided. We'll ride up and stay until sunset."

The others also stood. Sally, as usual, wanted to have the last word.

"Let's leave before sunset," she said. "You never know what the dark might bring."

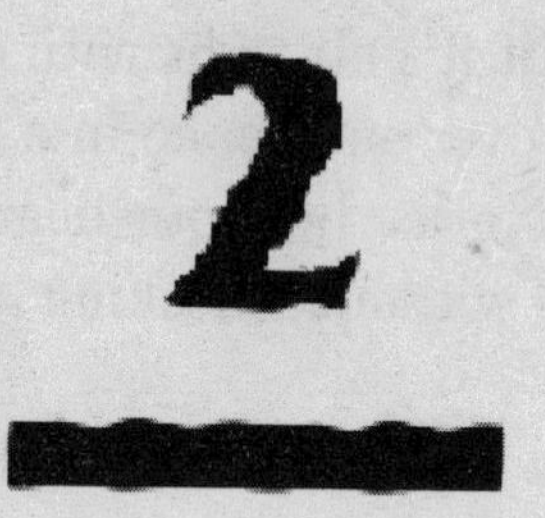

The bicycle ride up to the reservoir was harder than Adam had imagined. Even though they had to pedal on an incline most of the way, it was the temperature that really sapped Adam's strength. He was feeling wobbly when they arrived and climbed off their bikes. Fortunately, they had each brought a large plastic bottle of water.

"I feel a lot cooler now," Adam said sarcastically as he opened his bottle and held it up to his lips. "Now that we're here."

"It's like being in an air-conditioned mall," Cindy agreed, playing along and reaching for her water bottle. Her face was red from the sun and exertion.

"Give it a chance. It actually is cooler here," Watch said, stepping to the edge of the reservoir, which was a rough oval, maybe a quarter of a mile long and half that in width. The water was a strange gray color. The surrounding bank was almost entirely devoid of trees. All of their words seemed to die in the air the instant they left their mouths. Watch continued, "It's got to be at least ten degrees cooler."

"I feel refreshed from our ride," Sally said, although she had already plopped down on a boulder and drained half her water bottle. "I think my suggestion was a good one."

Cindy had brought a bag of sandwiches. Finding shade beneath one of the few trees, they sat down and ate. As they munched and talked and drank, Adam did begin to feel cooler. They had set off for the reservoir after four. It was now quarter to five and the heat was just beginning to ease up. But it was still too hot to do much exploring, not that any of them were in the mood to poke around another cave.

Watch had a pack of cards on him and wanted to play poker. Apparently Watch and Sally played together often. Adam was curious, although he had never played the game before and didn't know the rules. But Cindy was uneasy.

"My mother doesn't approve of gambling," Cindy said. "She says it's immoral and disgusting."

"Those two words fit me nicely," Sally said jokingly. "Listen, we're just going to gamble with pebbles. We start with twenty each. It's not really gambling unless you have real money at stake. I mean, how can your mother be upset if you lose a pile of rocks?"

Cindy chuckled. "You have a point. All right, I'll play as long as I don't have to wager my next week's allowance."

Watch explained the rules of five-card stud, and for the next hour or so they played many hands. But Watch and Sally were way ahead of Adam and Cindy when it came to the subtleties of the game. Adam and Cindy quickly lost all their pebbles, and even fierce Sally was steadily withering to Watch's apparent skill. She got down to five pebbles, but finally seemed to be holding a strong hand because she bet two of them at once. Watch was unmoved; he matched her bet.

"I think you're bluffing," he said confidently.

Sally caught his eye. "You think so, babe?" She

picked up the remainder of her pebbles. "I raise you another three. Count them."

Watch was unimpressed. "I still think you're bluffing."

Sally sneered. "Thoughts aren't rocks. Put your pebbles where your mouth is."

Watch coolly matched her bet.

Sally was momentarily taken aback.

"What have you got?" Watch asked.

Sally threw her cards down. "Trash. You win. Darn."

"It was an impressive bluff," Adam told Sally.

"I fell for it," Cindy agreed.

"It's not impressive unless it works," Sally muttered.

The sun was near the horizon and they were thinking of returning home when a minor disaster struck. Cindy, still curious about the Haunted Cave, had hiked up to peek at the opening to see if it was closed. They allowed her to go by herself because she had promised not to step inside if it was open. She was on her way back down the hill when she must have stepped on some loose gravel. The ground seemed to go out from under her before she started toppling.

"Cindy!" Adam shouted when he saw what was

happening. Sally and Watch looked over, and soon all three were running to Cindy. She hadn't toppled far, maybe twenty feet. But it was enough to pick up several scrapes and bruises. She was wearing shorts, and her legs were bleeding slightly in a few places. But that was not the major problem. As they reached her side, they saw her clutching her right ankle. Adam knelt by her side.

"Did you twist it?" he asked.

Cindy grimaced. "Yeah. It hurts."

"You didn't break it, did you?" Sally asked, concerned. "Your bone isn't sticking out, is it?"

"If you did break it, there won't be an ambulance coming for you," Watch said matter-of-factly. "Spooksville's ambulance drivers have all disappeared."

"Would you two shut up?" Adam said. "Can't you see she's in pain?"

Cindy forced a smile. "It's not too bad. I want to try putting some weight on it."

"You might want to ice it first," Watch suggested.

"Like we just happen to have bags of ice with us," Sally said sarcastically.

Adam helped Cindy up. The moment Cindy put

her right foot down, she let out a soft cry. "Ah," she said, breathing heavily. "It really hurts."

Adam pointed to the reservoir. "Maybe you should soak it in the water. It will help with the swelling."

"I wouldn't put my foot in that water if I'd just had sulfuric acid splashed on my toes," Sally said.

Watch strolled over to the water and crouched down. Before any of them could say a word, he reached over and cupped a handful of water. He raised it to his lips and swallowed, then nodded, satisfied.

"It could use a little fluoride, but otherwise it tastes fine," he said.

"We should wait a minute to see if he falls over dead," Sally whispered to Adam and Cindy.

Watch walked back to them. "I don't think it will melt your skin off, Cindy. But leave your shoe on when you put your foot in the water. The pressure of the sides of the shoe will help keep the swelling down as much as the cold water."

"OK," Cindy muttered as Watch and Adam helped her to a spot close to the water. Cindy sat down and added, "I feel like such a klutz, falling like that."

"I fell," Sally said proudly. "Once. But I regained my balance before causing myself any harm."

"Was the Haunted Cave open or closed?" Watch asked.

"It's still closed," Cindy replied, as she carefully placed her aching ankle into the water. "I didn't have the nerve to try to open it with one of the magic words we learned from the witch." She twitched. "Hey, this water is really cold."

"Some people say the reservoir is bottomless," Sally said. "None of the bodies dumped in here over the years has ever floated back to the surface."

"I think I'm going to talk my parents into buying a water purifier when I get home," Adam said. He clasped Cindy's hand and spoke in a gentle voice. "Is the pain letting up?"

"Oh, Watch," Sally said, touching her heart. "Look at his bedside manner. He's a born doctor. Dr. Adam—maybe he could be a brain surgeon."

"It feels better, thank you," Cindy said, ignoring Sally. "If I can just soak it for a few more minutes, I may be able to ride back home."

"You can ride a bike with one foot," Sally said. "Jaws does it all the time."

"He's David Green, the kid who lost a leg to the

great white shark who stays off our coast," Watch explained in case Adam or Cindy had forgotten.

"You're lucky there are no sharks in the reservoir," Sally added.

"We'll wait here until you feel ready to travel," Adam told Cindy.

Watch nodded toward the west. "The sun is setting. It'll be dark soon."

"This is what I was afraid would happen," Sally said. She took a step away from the water and sat back down. "There's no moon tonight. It will get black as ink up here."

3

Watch and Sally were both right. Not long after the sun left the sky, the stars started to come out. As the night deepened, the number of stars rose dramatically. Adam had never seen so many stars, nor had he ever really enjoyed the Milky Way before. The nebulous river of the galaxy stretched across the entire sky. Watch, who seemed to know a great deal about astronomy, pointed out the Northern Cross and told them about the blue-white star at the base of it.

"That's Deneb," he said. "It's tens of thousands of times brighter than our sun. I think it's the brightest star in the sky that we can see. It even has a red star that circles it, but you can't see that with the naked eye."

"But what about that one?" Sally asked, pointing straight overhead. "That one's several times brighter."

"That's Vega," Watch said. "It's twenty-six light-years away. It's also a lot brighter than our sun. But it's no Deneb. Deneb is thousands of times farther away than Vega. If Deneb was only twenty-six light-years from here, it would outshine anything else in the sky."

"How did you learn all these things?" Cindy asked, impressed.

Watch shrugged in the dark. They could hardly see one another. Each of them was just a black line drawn against the stars.

"I have a telescope at home," Watch finally answered. "And I study books on astronomy at the library. Mr. Spiney has a few good ones."

"Watch built his own telescope," Sally said, with a trace of pride in her voice.

Because they were enjoying the stars so much and listening to Watch's stories about the constellations, they hardly noticed the passage of time. Cindy had been soaking her foot for more than an hour when Adam suggested she try putting weight on it again. They helped her up, and gently she put it down. She started to tell them how it felt, but something remarkable interrupted her.

A strange light appeared in the sky.

"What the heck is that?" Sally gasped.

Straight overhead was a white light, much brighter than any star. At first it was just a point; they couldn't tell its size. But as they watched, it grew brighter, and they all got the impression that it was going to land on them. Then it just stopped and hovered far above.

"Is it a plane?" Cindy whispered.

"A helicopter can hover," Watch said. "Not a plane. But I don't think it's a helicopter. We'd be able to hear its rotor."

"Could it be a balloon?" Adam asked.

"It's not moving like a balloon," Watch said. "It swept down and then just stopped."

Sally chuckled uneasily. "Well, it's not a flying saucer, is it?"

There was a moment of silence.

"That's exactly what I think it is," Watch said finally.

"We should get out of here," Cindy said.

"I don't know," Adam said, getting excited. "I've

always wanted to see a UFO. Do you think it will land, Watch?"

Watch shrugged. "This is Spooksville. Where else would an alien feel so at home on Earth?"

Perhaps the occupants aboard the strange ship heard Watch. For right then it descended once more, dropping like a glowing meteor out of a black abyss. They saw then that they were staring at two vessels, not one. The ships had been flying so close together that their lights had blurred. Adam's excitement was blunted by fear. The lights changed from white glows to definite shapes. The objects were flying saucers, for sure, and they were coming down fast.

They clearly intended to land at the reservoir.

"Maybe we should go hide behind the rocks," Adam said quickly. "At least at first."

Watch considered for one second. "Good idea. Can you walk, Cindy?"

"I can hobble if you guys help me," she replied, fear in her voice. The saucers were now only a quarter mile overhead. Their brilliant white glow radiated out over the surface of the reservoir, turning it into one huge silver mirror. For a moment they halted again, apparently searching for a place to set down. Unfortunately a decision was made swiftly.

The UFO's were going to park near their bikes.

"Let's carry her!" Adam shouted as they stumbled slowly toward the large rocks behind which they hoped to hide.

"Good idea!" Watch shouted back.

They didn't even ask Cindy for permission. They just each grabbed a leg and yanked her up so that she was riding on their shoulders. Sally ran ahead of them, leaping from rock to rock. She was clearly visible; they all were. Behind them the saucers hovered no more than twenty feet above their bicycles. Incredibly, there was no noise, not even a faint hum.

"I hope they didn't see us," Adam gasped, as they carried Cindy around the largest boulder and set her down behind it. From above their heads, the glow stabbed past the edges of the rocks. Certain that Cindy was sitting comfortably, Adam, Sally, and Watch climbed back up the boulders to peer at the ships.

Both ships were landing beside the water, practically on top of their bicycles. One continued to glow brilliantly. The other must have turned off its engine or warp drive or whatever because it only gave off a feeble white glow, nothing more. Both ships were saucer shaped, circular, maybe thirty feet in diameter. Actually, they looked like saucers with cups placed upside-down on them. It didn't take a genius to know they were not from planet Earth.

"What's happening?" Cindy whispered, sitting below them.

"They're unloading an antimatter bomb and preparing to blow up the planet," Sally said.

"Quiet," Adam cautioned. "They're just sitting there. Nothing's— Wait! I think I see a door opening."

Adam was correct. On the ship that was no longer glowing brightly, a door of sorts was materializing. It was a peculiar opening. There had been no sign of it a few seconds ago. It was as if the walls of the ship had suddenly dissolved in a rectangular pattern. Yellow light shone out from inside. The door was not large; Adam would have had to stoop to enter the vessel.

"Do you see any aliens?" Adam asked.

"I'm the last person to ask," Watch said. "I'm half blind."

"I hope they're not disgusting looking," Sally whispered. "Even E.T. gave me nightmares."

"You can't think that way," Watch said. "They have probably traveled millions of miles to get here. They have evolved from an entirely separate genetic tree. We will probably look horrible to them."

"I think I look horrible to my own mother half the time," Sally muttered.

"Shh," Adam cautioned. "One of them is coming out."

Actually, two of them were exiting the flying saucer. They couldn't have looked more alien. Their skin was vaguely scaly, brown; their heads were huge relative to their tiny bodies. Their faces were V-shaped. Although their mouths and noses were tiny, their eyes were huge—black and almond-shaped. Their legs and arms were bony, but they had big hands, and what looked like only four fingers, no thumb. They wore thin tan jumpsuits and black belts that carried exotic tools. In their hands they appeared to carry weapons of some kind. They both looked around as they stepped from their ship. They were very alert.

"What's happening?" Cindy said from below them.

"They're as disgusting as I imagined they would be," Sally whispered.

"But they look friendly," Watch said.

"Watch!" Sally hissed. "They're carrying weapons."

"Probably only for protection," Watch said.

"Yeah, right," Sally said. "I bet they shoot first and ask questions later."

Watch shook his head. "They're obviously from a culture far more advanced than ours. I'm sure they've left mindless violence behind, and I want to talk to them."

"I don't know," Adam said quietly. "Their technology may be advanced, but that doesn't mean they're concerned about us. For all we know, they could be here to collect specimens. Watch, you've talked about that before. It might be better to stay out of sight, and just see what happens. Oh, look, the other ship's light has gone off. I think I see another door forming."

The second ship was also opening up. Another two aliens stepped from the saucer. They joined their buddies, who now stood by the water, beside the bicycles. The aliens gestured with their instruments at the bikes. They seemed to be carrying on a conversation but they weren't talking or making any other kind of sound. Adam remarked on that and Watch had an explanation.

"They probably communicate using telepathy," Watch said. "Exchanging thoughts directly from mind to mind."

"Do you think they can read our minds from here?" Sally asked, worried.

"Who knows?" Watch said. "I really want to make contact with them."

"Why?" Adam asked. "I think it's too risky."

Watch shrugged. "I want to go for a ride in one of their spaceships." He moved away from them. "You guys stay here."

Sally grabbed his arm. "Wait a second. They can see there are four bikes. They'll come looking for us, if they like the looks of you, or even if they don't like your looks. You're risking all of us with this idea."

Watch spoke seriously. "Why do we live in Spooksville? It's not just because our families live here. It's because this is a place of adventure. The unknown surrounds us every time we leave our homes. I know what I'm doing is dangerous. All great adventures are."

Cindy was impressed. "That was a nice speech, Watch."

"If they capture you and take you prisoner," Adam said, "I don't know if we'll be able to rescue you." He gripped his friend's hand. "If they take you inside their ship, we might never see you again."

There was still a faint glow from the saucers. They could see enough of Watch's face to read his expression. For a moment he seemed touched, an unusual emotion for him. Most of the time Watch showed as much emotion as, well, one of the aliens hanging out by the water.

"You'd miss me?" he asked, surprised.

"We would miss you terribly, you major idiot," Sally said.

"Be careful," Cindy called from below. "Don't take any risks."

"The only way you can do that in this town is to stay in bed twenty-four hours a day," Sally said. But she reached over and gave Watch a hug. "Don't let them do any genetic experiments on you. You're fine the way you are, really."

Adam shook Watch's hand. "Shout for help if you think you're in trouble."

"Just don't use our names," Sally added.

Watch said goodbye and slowly walked toward the reservoir. As soon as he was away from the rocks, the aliens noticed him and raised what appeared to be their weapons. From the reaction of the aliens, it didn't appear as if they knew Watch—or the rest of them—had been there. Adam said as much to Sally and Cindy, who had now crawled up the rocks so that she could see like the rest of them.

"That's probably true," Sally said. "But why is such an advanced race greeting Watch with pointed weapons?"

Adam was grim. "Especially when he's holding out his hands to show he's not armed. I don't like this."

"He's so brave," Cindy whispered, anxious.

"He's a fool," Sally remarked. "A brave fool."

The aliens may or may not have tried to communicate with Watch. From a distance of two hundred feet it was hard for the other three to tell. It did appear as if Watch tried to talk to them, but Adam and his friends couldn't hear the aliens' telepathic responses. For sure, the aliens did not lower their weapons. Finally, after a couple of minutes of inspecting Watch from all angles, one of the aliens grabbed his arm and led him toward the door of the first saucer. Watch's friends got the impression he was being dragged into the ship, even though Watch didn't appear to put up a fight. Sally and Adam and Cindy anxiously looked at one another.

"What are we going to do now?" Cindy asked.

"Well," Sally said, "he wanted to see the ship. Now he gets to see the ship."

"He wanted to go for a joyride in space," Adam countered. "He didn't want to be dissected." Adam shook his head. "We can't just sit here and do nothing."

"I have a bad feeling that we can do nothing against their ray guns," Sally said. "Maybe we should call the President of the United States."

"It will take us forever to get to a phone without being able to use our bikes," Adam said. "We have to save Watch ourselves." He started to get up. "I'm going to speak to the aliens."

Sally grabbed his arm and pulled him back down. "Like you're going to have more success than Watch? Can't you see what's going on here? These aliens are here to collect genetic material to microscopically implant in their DNA to enrich and regenerate their ancient and failing species."

"You can tell all that just by looking at them?" Cindy asked doubtfully.

Adam shook free of Sally's hold. "I don't want to walk out there any more than you want to. If you have a better plan, let me hear it."

Sally thought for a moment. "Nothing comes to me right away. But let's not act hastily. Let's wait and see what happens."

What happened next was nothing. Watch did not reappear. But two of the aliens left the area around the reservoir and hiked back into the hills not far from where Adam and his friends were crouched.

"They could be trying to circle around us," Sally said.

Adam nodded darkly. "We have to watch our backs. But if I am going to confront them, this might be the time, while they're at half strength."

"I can't let you go out there alone," Sally said.

"You can't come with me," Adam said. "Cindy's injured. Someone has to stay with her."

"I'd rather you didn't go down there alone," Cindy said. "Take Sally with you."

"I wasn't volunteering myself," Sally complained. "I was just speaking generically." She paused and frowned. "I suppose I could go with you, Adam. But I hate not having a plan of action. We'll probably be taken prisoner like Watch and dragged to a distant planet circling a dying sun where we'll be dumped in a sterile prison and sliced open with a burning laser beam. Why, we're lambs going to slaughter."

"You're not a lamb, Sally," Cindy said.

"I was speaking poetically," Sally said.

"Tell me what else to do," Adam said.

"I don't know what else to do," Sally snapped back. "I just know that you can't trust gross-looking aliens with hand phasers."

"They only have phasers on 'Star Trek,'" Cindy said.

"How do we know these guys didn't write the TV show?" Sally asked.

Adam spoke wearily. "We're getting nowhere with this arguing. I'm going down and demand that they release Watch. You can come if you want, Sally. But I don't think it's a good idea."

"You mean it's all right for you to be a hero and not me?" Sally asked, getting to her feet. "Really, Adam, you're a bit of a sexist. A girl can save the day just as easily as a boy." She glanced once more at the saucers. Only one alien was visible, near the door of the first ship, the door through which Watch had disappeared. "I wonder if there are boy aliens and girl aliens."

"I think that's the least of our worries right now," Adam said.

"You never know," Sally replied. She leaned over and patted Cindy on the back. "If we don't come back, and you do manage to escape, write a book about me when you grow up. The world has to know what it lost tonight."

Cindy was not in a joking mood. "I wish you guys plenty of luck."

Together, Adam and Sally crept from behind the rocks and walked slowly in the direction of the two saucers. The alien standing guard reacted quickly to their approach. Stepping toward them, he drew his weapon and pointed it at their heads. Adam and Sally immediately put up their arms. Up close, the alien was even more strange looking. It had no nails on its fingers, not a trace of hair on its body. Its huge black eyes were completely devoid of emotion or feeling. They were so cold they could have belonged to an insect. Adam felt a sinking feeling in his chest. He doubted that he'd be able to reason with the creature.

"Hello," Adam said. "We come in peace. We mean you no harm. My name is Adam. This is my friend, Sally. You have another friend of ours inside your flying saucer. His name is Watch. We just want him back. That's all we want."

"But we do have friends in high places," Sally added. "And they would avenge our deaths with great relish."

"Shh," Adam cautioned her. "I don't know if it understands us."

The alien just stared at them for a minute. Then it gestured with its hand weapon. It wanted them to walk into the flying saucer. Adam shook his head.

"No," Adam said. "We want our friend back. We don't want to go in your ship. Give him back to us and we won't bother you anymore."

"Yeah," Sally added. "And remember that you're a visitor to this planet. Show some manners, will you?"

Apparently the alien didn't like Sally's tone. It took a step forward and grabbed her right arm. She shook it off—the alien didn't appear to be that strong—but it immediately grabbed her again. It pointed its weapon directly between her eyes. Sally recoiled in terror. That was enough for Adam. He was through talking. No more Mr. Nice Human.

Adam launched himself at the alien.

The alien spun on him. Leveled its weapon.

Adam saw a flash of green light. Heard Sally scream.

Then everything went black.

5

For Cindy, watching Adam and Sally fight with the alien was the hardest thing she had ever done. Cindy knew from the start the battle was hopeless. It especially hurt that she could do nothing to help her friends. A second after the alien shot Adam, it turned its weapon on Sally. To her credit, Sally didn't turn and run. She tried to attack the alien. But the creature was too quick for her. The black instrument in its hand spurted another blast of green light, and Sally collapsed on the ground beside Adam.

Cindy didn't even know if either of them was still alive.

She didn't have long to grieve over her fallen pals. She heard sounds behind her, farther up the hill. The other two aliens were either returning to their ship or else closing in to take her captive. Sprained ankle or not, Cindy swore to herself she would not be taken without a fight.

Climbing to her feet, hobbling on one foot, she listened hard, trying to determine the course of the aliens. They did not appear to be coming directly toward her. Rather, they were following the path of a narrow valley that cut through the side of the hill where she was hiding. Actually, it was more of a ravine, cut by the winter rains. It was only a hundred feet off to her right. Cindy decided she would hide above the lip of the ravine, and shower down rocks on the aliens as they came by. If she could get hold of just one of their weapons, she thought, it would help to even out the fight.

Trying her best to move silently, Cindy half hopped and half dragged herself to the edge of the ravine. She got there none too soon. The two aliens were almost directly below her. After grabbing hold of a watermelon-sized rock, she lifted it over her head. There was faint background light from the two saucers, although both ships were in dim mode. It gave her something to see by, but it was poor shooting at best. As she let the first rock fly, she knew she'd need a miracle to hit anything.

There was a flash of green light.

Cindy blinked. Had she been shot?

No. Just the opposite.

Below her, the two aliens lay unconscious on the ground.

"But who shot them?" Cindy whispered out loud. Looking around, she didn't see another soul, human or alien. Briefly she wondered if she had imagined the green light. Or maybe her rock had hit them—both of them. Or perhaps one of their weapons had accidentally gone off when it struck the ground. It didn't really matter, she decided. She was taking their weapons now. She had fought with ghosts and Hyeets—she could handle aliens.

Cindy hobbled down to where the aliens lay. They appeared stunned, not dead. She could hear them breathing. Quickly she stripped off their black belts and tucked one gun in her own belt while keeping the other ready in her right hand. She didn't know how these particular guns were set, if they would stun or kill when she fired them.

But fire she would, as soon as she caught sight of the monster who had shot Adam and Sally.

Cindy made it back to her position behind the rocks. But there was no chance for her to rest because the alien and his partner were dragging Adam into the saucer. They couldn't be too strong because even though there were two of them, they were struggling with Adam's body. Cindy had no doubt they would come back for Sally in a minute. Unfortunately, they had Adam beside the saucer already.

Cindy had a moment of panic. The ship was two hundred feet away. She couldn't run there; she could hardly walk. On the other hand, she couldn't stand and start shooting, not without risking hitting Adam. But she had to do something and she had to do it now. People who went in that ship did not come out.

Cindy stood and took aim. But not directly at the aliens. She aimed for the saucer itself. Pulling the trigger, she felt no recoil but saw a narrow flash of green light. It hit the side of the craft, and made the aliens jump. For a moment they dropped Adam and pointed in her direction. They raised their own weapons. Cindy wondered if they took target practice on their home world, and whether their weapons were set to kill or stun.

The large rock beside her exploded.

Cindy dove for cover. But she was back up again in a moment, having crawled a few feet to the side. So they wanted to play rough. Cindy twisted a tiny knob on her weapon all the way around in the other direction. She didn't know what the knob controlled, but she figured it might boost the weapon's power. Again she took aim at the saucer and pulled the trigger.

Her ray gun was no longer set on stun.

The ship was alive with sparks as the green beam licked its surface. The hull of the saucer did not break, and Cindy guessed the ship was probably still capable of spaceflight. Cindy fired again, and got a similar violent response. But she had to be very careful not to aim at Adam or the aliens, who were terribly exposed. At least she had a ton of rocks to hide behind. They took another couple of shots at her and set a lot of dust flying, but they didn't come close to hitting her. They appeared anxious to get inside their spacecraft. Maybe they weren't used to humans who fought back.

Grabbing Adam, they yanked him into the saucer.

Before Cindy could get off a third shot, the door vanished.

"No!" Cindy screamed, jumping out from her place behind the rocks, almost falling over because of her bad ankle. The saucer began to glow brightly. She knew it was preparing for take off. Raising her weapon once more, she took aim. This time she fired off a series of shots in quick succession. The saucer shook under the pounding, and there were sparks and smoke everywhere. But Cindy should have realized that the saucer had weapons of its own. As it bobbled off the ground, it spun around and Cindy saw two green streaks rush toward each other along the perimeter of the ship. As they collided, a blinding beam of light flashed toward her. Cindy instinctively dove to the side and half the hill behind her flew into the air in one gigantic explosion.

The noise was deafening, the shock wave crushing. If Cindy hadn't been flat on the ground, she would have been killed. As it was, she lay stunned for several moments, recovering only when the saucer was a vanishing white dot in the sky. She opened her eyes just as it blinked out of view.

"They got Adam," she whispered. "They got Watch."

But they didn't get Sally. Cindy made her way to her friend, who lay unmoving not far from the remaining saucer. Smoke and tiny fires littered the landscape. Sally had a pulse, and she was breathing. Cindy hobbled to the water and soaked her shirt in it. Then she returned to Sally and squeezed the water onto her friend's face. Sally opened her eyes with a start.

"That better not be water from the reservoir," Sally said.

"It is," Cindy said.

Sally sat up and wiped her face with the back of her arm. "You better pray my face doesn't turn gray and my hair doesn't fall out," she complained. "Or else you're going to be bobbing for apples tomorrow night in a barrel of reservoir water."

"They've taken Adam and Watch," Cindy cried.

"Oh, my head hurts." Sally rubbed her forehead. "What are you talking about?"

"The aliens! Their ship left with Adam and Watch on it!"

Sally was instantly alert. She glanced around. "Why didn't they take me?"

Cindy held up one of her weapons. "I ambushed a couple of aliens and took their guns. They're lying over there in the ravine, unconscious." Cindy paused and gestured to the remaining flying saucer. "Why don't we drag them back to their ship, wake them up, put a gun to their heads, and demand that they go after Adam and Watch?"

Sally thought for a moment then smiled wickedly.

"Sounds like my kind of plan," she said.

When Adam came to, he was lying on his back. The first thing he felt—besides the floor beneath him—was his headache. He could hear his pulse in his head. It pounded like thunder. Every time his heart beat, it was as if the nerves in his brain squeezed together. He felt so awful he saw no point in even opening his eyes. But he did anyway.

"How are you doing?" Watch asked, sitting beside him. "Got a headache?"

Adam groaned. "Yeah. How did you know?"

"I had the same thing when I woke up. I felt like

my skull was about to explode. I think I got zapped by the same gun as you."

Right then Adam remembered the alien and his nasty weapon. He pulled himself into an upright position. It took a moment before his vision cleared enough for him to see straight. Then he immediately thought he was imagining things.

He was inside an alien craft flying through space. The ship was not large. From where he and Watch sat to the opposite side, where the two aliens stood at an exotic control panel, was only about twenty feet. Except for the controls, the interior was relatively featureless and rather dim. Adam had to squint to see clearly. The floor was covered with a simple tan carpet. The walls were off-white in color. The aliens had obviously not hired an interior decorator when they built their ship. At four spots around the walls was a small circular viewing screen.

Overhead there was a glorious sight. The ceiling appeared to be one huge viewing portal. Adam thought he had seen a lot of stars at the reservoir after the sun had gone down. There had to be a hundred times as many stars visible now. The Milky Way seemed to shimmer with a magical radiance. The unblinking stars seemed to be close enough to touch. He wondered if they had already left the solar system, and asked Watch. Watch shook his head.

"The ship changes orientation every few minutes," he said. "Not long ago I saw the sun through the ceiling. It's a lot smaller than we see it from Earth, but it's still there."

"Do you know where we're headed?"

"Your guess is as good as mine. But I'd assume we're returning to the aliens' home world."

"Do you think it's in our solar system?" Adam asked.

"No. There isn't another planet in our solar system that can support life. It has to be around another star. It may not even be in our galaxy."

"Great. What will we do there?" Adam said.

Watch shrugged. "I'm trying not to think about it."

Adam nodded to the two aliens, who appeared to be ignoring them. "Have they spoken to you?"

"No. They act like I'm not even here. But I'm convinced they're telepathic. They communicate strictly in silence."

"Do you think they can read our minds?" Adam asked.

"I'm not sure. If they can, I think they have to concentrate on picking up our thoughts. That's just an impression I get."

"How come they haven't tied us up?" Adam asked.

"We don't exactly have a lot of places to run away to."

"You have a point there," Adam agreed.

"Also, I think one blast of their guns was enough to tell us who's in charge. Is your head feeling any better?"

Adam rubbed his neck. "Yeah, it's getting there."

"The pain goes away pretty quick once you're awake."

Adam remembered something. "You know, just before I was shot, one of the aliens was wrestling with Sally. I wonder how she got away."

"Maybe she didn't. Maybe she's on board the other ship."

"Have you seen it?" Adam asked.

"No. But I assume it isn't far behind us."

Adam lowered his voice. "Do you have an escape plan?"

"No."

"You must have some ideas?"

Watch shook his head. "Neither of us knows how to pilot this ship. We can't forcibly take it over, even if they gave us half a chance. We're stuck."

"But I don't want to live the rest of my life on an alien planet."

"The rest of your life might not be that long."

"You're encouraging," Adam complained.

"I'm sorry. I just can't imagine how we're going to get out of this. Unless the aliens decide to take us back home. But I don't think that's likely. Not after they went to so much trouble to kidnap us."

"Did they stun you as soon as you went in the ship?"

"No. Only when I tried to leave." Watch nodded as if impressed. "They've got pretty cool guns. I wonder under what scientific principle they work."

Just then a circular door appeared in the center of the floor, and a small alien riding a narrow elevator appeared. He could have been a kid, although as far as Adam knew he might be ten thousand years old. Like the others, he had a huge head, but his large black eyes didn't seem as cold. He stared at them for a moment and then walked over to them. He bowed slightly as he stopped near their feet. He couldn't have been more than two feet tall.

"Hello," Adam said flatly. "What's your name? Or do you just have a number?"

To Adam's immense surprise, a reply immediately formed in his mind. It was not a thought of his own. The texture and clarity of it was much sharper. It was almost as if a miniature being had crawled inside his brain and shouted something out loud. The unspoken words definitely came from the creature in front of them.

"My name is a combination of syllables and numbers. I am Ekwee12. Who are you?"

Adam had to take a deep breath. The reply had startled yet also pleased him. He had not been looking forward to spending the rest of his days with mute aliens.

"I'm Adam, and this is my friend Watch."

The alien continued to stare at him with his flat eyes. His face showed no emotion.

"What is your number?"

"We don't have numbers where we come from," Adam said.

"What is your rating, then?"

"We don't have ratings either." Adam added, "But I'll be in seventh grade next year. Hopefully."

"I don't think they have junior high where we're heading," Watch muttered.

The alien glanced at Watch.

"What is junior high?"

"It's a type of school," Adam said. "It means you're too old to play with toys, but not old enough to drive a car."

"What is a car? A vehicle of transportation?"

"Yes," Adam said. "We have them where I live." He nodded to the other two aliens, who continued to ignore them. "How are you related to those two guys?"

"They are teachers. This is an educational trip for me."

Adam spoke bitterly. "Are they teaching you how to kidnap innocent people?"

The alien hesitated. For a moment the skin around his mouth seemed to wrinkle. He glanced at the aliens behind him and then back at them.

"Explain the word kidnap?"

"It means we have been taken against our wills," Adam said. "Your teachers knocked us out with their weapons. I was dragged unconscious aboard this ship. Didn't you see any of this happen?"

Again the alien paused. He seemed to be thinking.

"No. I was told to stay below after we landed."

"But you believe our story, don't you?" Adam

asked. For he sensed that the little alien did not approve of what had been done. Once more the alien took a moment before answering.

"You do not appear to be lying."

"We're telling you what happened," Watch said. "We were attacked by your people."

"You are not hurt."

"But we are being held captive," Watch said. "We want to go home."

"We are going home."

"We want to go to *our* home," Adam said. "Back to where we were picked up." He paused. "Can you help us?"

The little alien lowered his head. *"I am just a student. I am not in charge here."*

"But maybe you could talk to your teachers," Adam said. "Explain to them that we are upset."

The little alien glanced over his shoulder. *"They would not listen."*

Adam was curious. "Are they listening to us now?"

The little alien closed his eyes briefly. This was the first time they had seen his eyelids. They were faintly translucent, pretty weird looking. When he opened his eyes again, Adam thought he saw a faint spark in those black depths.

"No. They are not listening. They do not care about you two. Also, among my people, the young are better telepaths. My telepathic range is twice theirs."

"That's interesting," Adam said. "I thought it would have been the other way around. Why are kids better at picking up and sending thought?"

"We have less stress."

"We seem to be picking up speed," Watch said. "But even going this fast, I don't see how we're going to reach your home planet in the next century. Can you explain how this craft works?"

"This ship first accelerates to near light speed. Then we convert our momentum to pure energy and use the power to jump through hyperspace. We can only make such a jump far from the gravitational pull of your sun."

"Can we cross many light-years in a single hyperjump?" Watch asked.

The alien hesitated as if for once he did not understand the question. *"Yes. We can travel any distance, if it is necessary."*

"What does all this mean?" Adam asked Watch.

"That we're in serious trouble," Watch replied. "If we don't reverse our course before the hyperjump, I doubt we'll ever get home."

"When do we jump through hyperspace?" Adam asked the little alien.

The alien consulted a small instrument fastened to his wrist. *"Fifteen of your minutes."*

Adam was aghast. "That's so soon." He tried to keep his voice steady, yet he spoke with passion. "Do you care about us? Can you help us escape?"

The little alien may have tried to smile then because the tan flesh around his tiny narrow mouth creased. He probably shouldn't have bothered. His expression looked anything but friendly. But Adam sensed his good intentions.

"I care that your free will may have been violated. That is against the laws of our people. I do not understand how our teachers could have committed such a violation."

"You should point that out to them," Watch suggested.

But the alien repeated his earlier comment. *"They would not listen."*

Adam was sympathetic. "Adults don't listen to kids on your world either? It's the same where we come from. We have plenty of smart things to say but we're not even allowed to vote for president of our country." Adam paused. He spoke in a whisper. "Do you know how to fly this ship?"

"Yes."

"Can you help us escape?" Adam asked again, not wanting to push the guy but worried about the upcoming jump. "We really have to get home. My mother's already made me dinner by now. She'll be wondering where I am."

The little alien seemed to understand.

"I have a mother as well. She is nice to me." The alien glanced once more at his companions. He seemed lost in thought, or perhaps he was confused. He sent them a final mental communication. *"I will have to consider the situation."*

The alien turned and stepped to where the others stood. They acknowledged his arrival with a slight nod of their two fat heads, but if they communicated with the little guy Adam and Watch didn't hear it, with their ears or their minds. Adam continued to fret about the upcoming hyperjump.

"What do you know about hyperspace?" he asked Watch.

Watch shrugged. "Our scientists only have theories that it exists. But it sounds like this ship is capable of sliding into a shortcut through space. That's what hyperspace must be. This ship uses the energy of its tremendous speed to open the door to the shortcut."

"Then we have to brake somehow," Adam said.

"You can throw one of your shoes at the control panel, but I don't think that will do the trick," Watch said. "It will probably just get you shot again. And this time they might not have their guns on stun."

Adam started to stand. "I'm tired of sitting here doing nothing. I'd rather go down fighting."

Watch grabbed his arm. "We have to be patient. The little guy clearly wants to help us. Let's give him a chance."

Adam reluctantly sat back down. "I'll give him ten minutes, that's all."

But Adam didn't have to wait that long. Five minutes later the other flying saucer suddenly appeared. They saw it through the transparent ceiling. It swooped dangerously close, glowing brightly, and as it did an angry burst of green light struck the ceiling. For a moment Adam and Watch were blinded. Their own flying saucer shook violently as the lights dimmed more. Adam thought he smelled smoke.

The two aliens at the controls gestured excitedly, although they didn't say a word. They probably couldn't speak if they wanted to. Yet they had radio communications. Adam and Watch knew that for a fact a minute later when they heard Sally's voice come through the hidden speakers.

"This is Captain Sara Wilcox and Lieutenant Cindy Makey of the *Starship UFO.* We demand your complete and unconditional surrender. You have two Earth minutes to comply. Failure to do so will result in your immediate and total destruction."

Adam and Watch looked at each other in amazement.

Aboard *Starship UFO*—the ship's title as well as their respective ranks had been Sally's idea—Cindy wondered if Sally had pushed it too far. Behind them, against the far wall, the two aliens huddled together as if afraid. Cindy worried that they knew something their human enemies did not.

"Maybe we should negotiate a trade of prisoners," Cindy said.

"This is interstellar war," Sally said, her finger on the firing button. "I don't negotiate."

"But if you blow up their ship, you'll kill Adam and Watch," Cindy pointed out.

Sally removed her finger from the firing button. They had figured out how to work the weapons—and navigate the vessel—on the journey out from the sun. Of course the aliens had given them a few practical hints when Sally held the guns to their heads. Sally was showing the aliens no mercy. She was constantly yelling at them and threatening to boot them out into space, where they would surely die. Cindy did not approve of the cruelty, even though the aliens would probably have killed them if given the chance.

"I know that," Sally said. "But I have to bluff with conviction. If I don't, Adam and Watch will never escape."

"You don't know that for sure. A gentle approach might be better."

Sally shook her head. "Look who we're dealing with. These aliens land on our planet and immediately whip out their guns and kidnap our friends. We have to meet force with force. It's the only way."

"Did it ever occur to you that the aliens in the other ship have a thousand times more experience in interstellar combat than we do? What if they blow us out of the sky?"

Sally nodded. "I thought of that. That's why I hit them hard first. I'm hoping we've already disabled their weapons system."

Cindy pointed to the large viewing screen above. "You better pray as well as hope. They're coming around. And from the green glow around their perimeter, it looks like they're getting their weapons ready."

Sally spun on the aliens with a gun in her hand. "How do we raise our shields?" she demanded.

The aliens looked at each other with their huge insect eyes. They shook their heads slightly. They trembled as they did so, and hugged each other close. They had earlier communicated telepathically, but now they seemed too scared to send a clear thought.

"I think they're saying we don't have any shields," Cindy said.

"We have to have shields!" Sally shouted. "This is a spaceship. They always have shields in the movies."

A hard blast, thick as a fist, struck their ship. Sally and Cindy went flying and hit the floor. For a moment their lights failed and they were plunged into total darkness. It was terrifying; they could have been floating in empty space without a ship around them. Fortunately an emergency system came on, flooding the interior with a sober red light. Sally and Cindy crawled to their knees. Cindy felt a twinge in her right ankle. In all the excitement she had almost forgotten she was still injured.

"They'll pay for that," Sally said bitterly. She reached for the control panel, the firing button. "We're taking no prisoners."

Cindy stopped her. "Wait a second. I hear something."

"What?" Sally demanded.

"A telepathic message. Listen, here it comes again."

"Push the green button. Then the purple one."

"Did you hear that?" Cindy asked.

"Yeah. So what?" Sally pointed to the two quivering aliens, whose big black eyes seemed to be ready to burst from their heads. "They're just giving us instructions to blow ourselves up."

Cindy got to her feet. "They're more afraid of dying than we are. The thought's not coming from them. It must be coming from the other ship."

Sally was disgusted. "Like we're going to listen to an order from them? Are you out of your mind? I say we return fire. If we lose Adam and Watch then at least they died in a good cause." Once again she reached for the firing button. "I'm locking on all our weapons. I'm going to maintain fire until one of us explodes."

Cindy stopped her again. "That's insane. We're not killing Watch and Adam, and you know it. You're just raving." She suddenly paused and went still. "This thought feels different from the others. The person sending it seems to want to help us."

Sally threw her arms in the air. "The person sending the message is an alien! We can't trust it!"

Cindy spoke firmly. "And we can't just keep blasting away. I say we give this message a chance. I know that sounds insane but I trust it somehow."

Sally turned away in disgust. She glanced up at the ceiling. The other ship was coming around again. Sally could see them energizing their weapons.

"If you're going to respond to it, then you better do it now," Sally grumbled.

Cindy stepped over to the control panel and pushed a green button, then a purple one. There was only one button of each color on the panel. At first nothing seemed to happen. The other ship continued to bear down on them, its powerful weapons batteries glowing with a deadly green light. Then behind Cindy, Sally let out a gasp. Cindy whirled around to see a little alien standing in the center of their ship.

"Where did you come from?" Cindy exclaimed.

"You just teleported me from the other ship. I am here to help you, and your friends, Adam and Watch. May I use the control panel, please?"

"No!" Sally shouted, pointing her gun at the little alien. "We're not turning over our ship to a runt like you."

The alien stared at her calmly.

"I understand your lack of trust. I apologize for what my teachers have done so far to you and your friends. It is against our laws to infringe the free will of other intelligent creatures. I am here to help set the situation right. To do so, you must let me send a signal to the other ship. They will think I have taken control of this vessel and they won't fire upon it again. But if you don't let me take control, this ship will be destroyed in the next ten of your seconds."

"Let him do it!" Cindy cried.

"No!" Sally argued. "It could be a trap!"

"We're already trapped!" Cindy shouted back. She glanced overhead. The other ship was at the same distance as when it last fired. "We have no choice, Sally. Can't you see that? Lower your gun."

Sally hesitated, then turned angrily away. "This is your call, Cindy. If you're wrong, I'm never going to let you live it down."

"If I'm wrong, you and I won't be alive to live anything down." Cindy nodded to the little alien, who waited patiently in the center of the floor. "Do what you have to do. Hurry!"

The alien stepped up to the control panel. He pressed a series of buttons. Outside, above them, the other ship suddenly veered off. Cindy let out a cry of relief, but Sally was far from happy. She pointed a finger at the little alien.

"I want our friends released right now," she said. "Then I want you to take us back to Earth."

The little alien stared at them as he spoke in their minds.

"That is not possible right now. I have no control over what my teachers on the other ship may do. In a few of your minutes they plan to jump through hyperspace and return to our home world. It is my suggestion that you allow me to follow them."

"What?" Sally cried, raising her weapon once more. "Do you think we're that primitive that we'll fall for such a trick? If we go through hyperspace—

whatever that is—we'll never get home. You turn this ship around right now. We're returning to Earth."

"Sally, you have to control your temper," Cindy said. "It clouds your reasoning. We can't go home yet. We have to go where Adam and Watch go. You know that. You would be the last person to desert them. And I trust this little guy." She spoke directly to the alien. "When we reach your home world, do you think we can get our friends released?"

The alien hesitated.

"It is possible. I have a plan. But it is a dangerous plan."

Sally shook her head. She continued to point her gun at the alien. "Why should we trust you?" she demanded. "Why would you betray your own kind to help us?"

"I do not betray my own kind by doing what is right. If my teachers are breaking our laws, then I am helping them by calling the criminal act to their attention. Also, I have studied your kind since I was very young. I have always admired you. I wish only to be of service."

"A likely story," Sally muttered. She glanced at

Cindy. "How can you trust a runt with such a fat head?"

Cindy reached over and patted the little alien on the head. The guy seemed to enjoy the attention. He moved a step closer to her, and touched her leg with his funny four-fingered hand.

"I don't know, I think he's kind of cute," Cindy said. "In a strange way, he reminds me of Adam."

Sally snorted. "If we get out of this, I'm going to tell Adam you said that."

The alien looked at both of them.

"I think Adam would be happy to be compared to me."

The situation was desperate. They were lost in space with aliens from another planet, and their friends were being held captive. But both Sally and Cindy suddenly burst out laughing. They could just imagine what Adam would say to that.

For Adam and Watch the jump through hyperspace proved unremarkable. They were racing into deep space—with the sun now a bright star far behind them—when the aliens pushed a few buttons and there was a low hum. It lasted for only an instant. Adam felt as if everything went momentarily black. He felt a slight jerk; he might have twitched. Then he blinked and everything was exactly as it was before, only now the bright star was in front of them instead of behind them.

"I thought the scenery might have changed more," Adam muttered.

"So did I," Watch said, puzzled.

"Are we sure we made the jump through hyper-space?"

"It seems so. Something did happen." Watch studied the stars through the wide ceiling panel. "Maybe their solar system is not so far from our solar system, after all. Many of the constellations still look the same."

"Are they the same?" Adam persisted.

"No. There are definite changes. For example, the Big Dipper is bent out of shape. We must be seeing it from another angle. We have definitely traveled several light-years in the last few seconds. But . . ." Watch trailed off.

"But what?"

Watch shook his head. "I don't know what it is. Something is off here. I wish we still had our little friend to ask questions. I wonder where he went."

"I get the impression he was teleported to the other ship. Notice how he stood real still in the exact center of the floor. It was like he sent a mental signal to the girls to pick him up. Remember how he said his telepathic abilities had greater range than the adult aliens?"

"Do you think he's working for us?" Watch asked.

"I hope so. Hey, that was pretty cool the way Sally just opened fire."

"Yeah, it must have been her. She sure has guts. But she almost got us killed. I hope they follow us through hyperspace."

"So do I," Adam agreed. "I think the little alien is our only ally in this part of the universe."

Time crept by slowly. Adam and Watch began to feel hungry and thirsty. They complained to their captors but were completely ignored. Adam talked again about trying to jump the aliens, but he was now too tired to make the effort. Plus the more time that went by, the more he began to believe that the little alien was definitely in the other ship, and following them. Unfortunately they could see no sign of the other vessel. Perhaps that wasn't important. It was a big universe. The ship would have to be extremely close to be visible.

The sun up ahead continued to grow in brilliance. When it was about the same size as the sun as seen from Earth, they saw a blue-white planet, around which a silver moon circled. At first glance Adam thought he was seeing the Earth, but a closer look showed him that the continents and oceans were nothing like those at home. He felt a stab of despair. Even in the Haunted Cave, when everything had looked hopeless, he had still been able to make decisions that had at least affected their destiny. Here he was completely helpless. He had only a kid alien to depend on. Beside him, Watch pointed in the direction of the planet.

"See those glittering silver shapes orbiting the planet?" Watch said. "I think each of them is either a space station or a spaceship. This culture must be extremely advanced. Some of them look huge."

"Maybe they all live in space," Adam suggested. "Maybe they polluted their planet so bad they can't live on the ground."

"The way the human race is going, that might happen to us," Watch said.

"If this alien race doesn't destroy us first," Adam said. "I've been thinking of the bigger picture. Our lives may not be all that is at stake here. What if they're preparing a huge invasion of our planet? What if they kidnapped us so they can torture us for what we know?"

"But we don't know anything," Watch said.

"That's true, but they wouldn't know that. For all they know, kids from Spooksville may be the ruling class on planet Earth."

"We certainly have seen more weird things than anybody else back home." Watch continued to stare at the approaching planet, and the silver chain of floating spaceships and space stations. "Your pollution theory might not be farfetched. See that brown murky junk near that coast?"

"Yeah."

"That looks like smog to me. Really bad smog. It's amazing, for all their advanced technology, that they haven't been able to clean it up."

"It's easier to prevent a spill than to clean one up," Adam said philosophically. "But personally I don't care how messed up their world is. I just want to get home and have dinner."

"Turkey and mashed potatoes would be nice right now," Watch agreed.

"Is that what your aunt was cooking tonight?" Adam knew Watch didn't live with either of his parents, or even with his little sister. But he had never asked his friend why the family was not together. The subject seemed too touchy. Watch lowered his head at the question.

"My aunt never cooks," he said softly. "I have to prepare all my own food."

Adam reached over and patted him on the back. "You can come to my house any time for dinner. You're always welcome."

Watch smiled faintly. "You only tell me that now that your house is billions of miles away."

Adam had to chuckle. "Listen, how did you know for sure Sally was bluffing? She acted exactly as if she had a strong hand."

"The cards are marked."

Adam was shocked. "What? You mean you cheated?"

"Sort of."

"But that's terrible. Why play if you're going to cheat?"

"Even with my glasses, I can't see people's expressions as well as you guys can. So I mark the cards just to make it even."

"How can you see the marks if you can't see our faces?"

"You forget, I was dealing. I do it really just to even the odds."

"Oh," Adam said. "When you explain it that way, I guess it isn't really cheating."

"You can have your rocks back if you want."

"That's all right. I'm not into rocks."

Watch pointed out one of the small viewing screens on the walls. "See that huge cylindrical station? I think that's our destination. Would you look at the size of it? The station must be twenty miles long."

Watch was right; the alien station was breathtaking in its size and sophistication. It was like a miniature world. And the most amazing thing was that there were thousands of others just like it in orbit.

The station rotated on its axis. But the flying saucer, as it approached, didn't try to match the station's speed—not exactly. It seemed as if they would enter the station from the top, in the center, where there was no obvious movement at all. Before them, a wide black door suddenly materialized. Adam was reminded of a hungry mouth, ready to swallow them. The saucer moved toward it. He shook his head sadly.

"Even if the little alien is helping us," he said. "I don't see how he can get us out of here."

"It does look hopeless," Watch agreed. "But it usually does when you live in Spooksville."

"We're a long way from Spooksville," Adam grumbled.

The saucer flew inside. For a moment all was dark. Then they exited into a massive chamber lit with soft yellow light. The wide space was a parking lot for saucers just like the one they were in. Literally hundreds of them floated nearby. Smoothly, their pilot maneuvered past the others. They seemed to be headed toward a dock of some kind. Adam knew they would be leaving the ship in a minute. The fact deepened his depression. At least, inside the spaceship, they had always had the chance of turning around and going home. Now that didn't seem possible.

There was a soft bump and then the ship went completely still.

A door materialized off to their left.

It led into a seemingly endless hallway.

The two aliens turned and drew their weapons.

The message was clear—get up and get going.

Adam and Watch stood slowly.

"Are we having fun yet?" Adam asked.

"Sure," Watch said. "So much fun we might die laughing."

The aliens escorted them from the flying saucer.

Sally and Cindy had indeed followed Adam and Watch through hyperspace. With the little alien's help, they stayed far enough away to remain invisible. Yet Cindy believed the aliens on Adam's ship thought the control of *her* ship had been returned to the aliens—the two cowards Sally had finally locked belowdecks. Their pal had given them that impression. He was acting the part of the hero in the fight between aliens and humans. Yet, as much as Cindy trusted him, she worried that Sally might be right. Maybe he was simply leading them into a trap.

Yet he seemed so sincere. As they plowed toward his home world, he asked so many questions. It seemed he had been studying them since he was old enough to read.

"Why were you up in the hills by the water?"

"We were trying to cool off," Cindy said. "It's been hot in our hometown lately. We rode our bikes up to the reservoir. Did you see them?"

"No. Just before landing, my teachers made me go below."

"They just didn't want you to see how cruel they are," Sally muttered.

"That may be true, and if it is, I am disturbed. A report to our government must be made. The people must know what is happening."

Sally snorted. "On our world, if you make a report to the government, it takes forever to hear about it. It's much quicker to get on TV."

"I know your TV. I have studied it. You watch different shows. Some of them involve space travel, although your race is not yet advanced to travel much farther than Earth orbit."

"We've been to the moon," Cindy said. "We might go to Mars soon."

"If you know about our TV," Sally said, "you must have seen programs on you guys. We know about aliens. We know you float down in the middle of the night and mutilate our cattle and steal our children. You can't underestimate us. If you try to invade, we won't be taken by surprise."

The little alien paused and stared at her.

"I am not an alien. Do you not know that?"

Cindy spoke quickly. "What Sally means is that you appear alien to us. I'm sure on your home world you look just fine. There, we would be the aliens."

"You would not be alien to us. That is not possible."

"Then your people must be more accepting than ours," Cindy said.

"They sure aren't any less violent," Sally grumbled.

The alien lowered his head.

"My people are not perfect. We have our problems."

Time went by. Up ahead, the alien sun continued to grow in size as they flew toward the heart of the solar system. About three hours after making the hyperjump, they caught sight of a blue-white world. Cindy and Sally were surprised to see it had a moon just like their own circling it. For a moment the girls wondered if they hadn't simply flown in a huge circle. But that wasn't the case; they were far from home. Studying the planet, they didn't recognize a single one of the continents.

The little alien steered them toward a huge space station.

"Are you sure this is where Adam and Watch were taken?" Cindy asked as they neared the massive structure.

"Yes."

"How do you know?" Sally demanded.

"I was informed by what you call radio."

"Can the two aliens we have stowed below deck communicate telepathically with your government and warn them that we have taken over your ship?" Sally asked.

"I have erected a mental shield around this ship. I have set it so that only my thoughts are allowed in and out."

"What do your people intend to do with Adam and Watch?" Cindy asked.

The huge space station was very near. They were coming in at the top. A black doorway opened before them.

"I do not know."

"What did your teachers tell you was their reason for going to Earth?" Sally asked.

"They said we went there to observe. To learn."

The ship slowed to a crawl. They began to enter the station.

"Well, I hope they learned not to mess with us," Sally replied. "You said you had a plan to rescue our friends. What is it?"

"It is hard to explain."

Sally fingered the weapon she kept tucked in her belt. "You're going to have to do better than that. I have trusted you this far, but before I leave this ship I want to know what you have up your sleeve."

The alien appeared puzzled. He checked his sleeve.

"I have nothing up it except my arm, Sally."

Sally snorted. "Just tell me how we're going to get our friends out of this metal cylinder."

The alien thought for a moment.

"None of us is going to leave this ship. Not right now. I am going to try to start what you call a riot."

"What?" Cindy gasped.

"I am going to broadcast the thought that your friends have been taken by force and are being held captive. I have explained that this act violates our most important laws. But I can only do this once I know where your friends are, and once I am hooked into what you would call a youth computer network. Except this network works with telepathy, not elec-

tric modems such as you have in your present-day culture."

Sally glanced at Cindy. "Did you get all that?" Sally asked.

"I don't know." Cindy spoke to the alien, "Why do you first have to know where Adam and Watch are?"

"Young people play pranks in our culture as they do in your culture. I will have to prove that your friends are being held captive. The best way to do this is to direct as many individuals my age as possible to the place where Adam and Watch are."

"What if they are in a restricted area?" Sally asked.

"Nowhere in our culture is supposed to be restricted."

"Why do you have to be hooked up to a network?" Sally demanded. "Why can't you just broadcast the information with your fat head . . . I mean, just with your incredible telepathic abilities?"

"It is easier on the network. It is set up so that interference is filtered out. I will be able to reach many more people this way."

"When you say a riot do you mean that hordes of your kind will begin to loot and burn?" Sally asked.

The idea seemed to startle the alien. He took a moment to respond.

"No. I mean that my people will gather and demand that Adam and Watch are released. It is the only plan I can think of."

Sally glanced at Cindy and shook her head. "I think our little friend underestimates what his government has going on the side."

"What do you mean?" Cindy asked.

"Think about it. These ships obviously landed in Spooksville with the purpose of taking hostages. The aliens we hijacked weren't there to explore. They were there to grab humans, pure and simple. That means they must have done it before, many times."

"What are you saying?" Cindy asked.

"I am finally beginning to believe this runt is on our side. But I think he is naive—his government is up to all kinds of secret stuff that he knows nothing about. That's why his teachers hid him out of the way when we were being kidnapped. Ten to one he's never going to be able to find out where Adam and Watch have been taken, especially if he stays inside this ship." Sally paused and spoke to the alien. "Did you hear that? What is your name anyway?"

"Ekwee12."

"Do you mind if I call you Ek?" Sally said. "No? Good. Did you hear what I just said?"

"Yes."

"Well, what do you think?"

"I hope you are wrong."

Sally had to laugh, but it was not a happy laugh. "You can hope all you want. But I think we'll all be lucky to get out of this alive. One thing for sure. As soon as we dock, there will be a group of guards waiting outside for us."

"No. I have already sent a message ahead that I have taken control of this ship. That is what I told my teachers on the other ship that I was going to do. There will be no guards waiting for us."

"Ek, I hate to tell you this," Sally said. "But you're about to get your first lesson in the real universe. This ship fired on the other ship. That is no small matter. Guards will be waiting for us and they will be armed. As soon as we dock I want you to let them in. Cindy and I are going to be hidden behind. As soon as we see them, we're going to stun them and lock them up with the other goons. In fact, set our guns to the right setting. I don't want to kill the guards accidentally. I would feel bad about it afterward."

Ek had to put a hand to his head.

"You will just shoot them if they come in?"

"Yes," Sally said. "Listen, one of your guys already shot me once. And I woke up with a splitting headache. I have a right to a little retaliation."

Ek gestured in front of them.

"We are about to dock. I should be able to tap into the network from here. I hope you are wrong about all this, Sally."

10

Adam and Watch were first led to a locker room where they were told—telepathically—to undress and shower under a strange orange liquid. Actually, after all the bike riding and alien fighting, the shower was rather pleasant. The liquid was warm and smelled nice. Adam was happy to wash the dirt out of his hair.

But while they were in the shower their clothes were taken. In their place were laid out two tan jumpsuits similar to the ones the aliens wore, only larger. This was OK with Adam and Watch; neither of them was particularly attached to his clothes. They dressed quickly, enjoying the feel of the soft material against their skin. The only trouble was Watch's glasses were missing. He stumbled around the room while Adam looked for them. The two guards just stood like statues, holding their ray guns. Finally Adam got fed up.

"All right," he said. "What did you do with my friend's glasses? He needs them. He can't even walk down a hall without them."

At first the aliens acted as if they didn't understand. They gestured with their guns for Adam and Watch to exit by a door on the far side of the room. But Adam refused.

"We are not going anywhere until he gets his glasses back." Adam pointed to his own eyes, then pointed at Watch's eyes. "Understand? He uses those things to see."

The aliens gestured again with their guns.

"No." Adam crossed his arms over his chest. "You're going to have to shoot us both. We are not leaving without those glasses."

"Maybe you should tell them that they can shoot you if they want," Watch said, as he bumped into a wall.

But the ultimatum worked. Finally they received a telepathic message.

"We did not know the glasses were so important."

The glasses were returned and they were led from the locker room area to a small cubicle that was equipped with an Earth-like toilet and two small beds set near the floor. The far wall of the room was made of what looked like clear glass or plastic; they could see through it into what appeared to be a courtyard. The moment they were inside the tiny room, the aliens turned and left, locking the door behind them. Adam pounded on it for several seconds before giving up in frustration. There wasn't even a doorknob he could try to jimmy or break.

"This is a cage," Adam muttered.

"It's one of many cages," Watch said, standing near the far wall. "Look out there."

Around the circular courtyard were twenty such rooms. Each was equipped with a similar transparent wall and held a different creature from other worlds. Some cells held two of the same species. In one glance, Adam and Watch were treated to an overview of many life forms from other galaxies.

Closest to them was a critter that had six heads.

Six feet tall, it was vaguely insectile; it walked on six legs and had dozens of eyes on three of its heads. On the remaining three were tiny claws and mouths. It stared at them wickedly, snapping its claws repeatedly. Adam and Watch instinctively backed away from their transparent wall. The thing looked as if it wanted to eat them.

In another cage was a bloblike being that flowed from one corner of its container to another. There were fish creatures, birdmen, and even one individual that looked like a cross between a robot and a dinosaur. They saw what they thought was a Hyeet—a Bigfoot. The hairy apelike fellow waved to them. Adam waved back without enthusiasm.

"We're in a zoo," he said miserably.

"I wonder," Watch said. "Where are all the tourists?"

"Maybe it's nighttime."

"You wouldn't have a specific nighttime aboard a space station. People would probably work in shifts, around the clock. If this is a zoo, I think it would have to be open all the time."

"What are you saying?" Adam asked.

Watch scratched his head. The aliens had taken his four watches and hadn't returned them with his glasses. Adam knew how much his friend must miss them. They were like a part of his body, his persona even. Of course, if there was no night and day on a space station, then there were no time zones either. Watch had an accepting nature and hadn't complained of the theft.

"I think this is more of a laboratory," Watch said finally. "I think we're cut off from the public."

Adam frowned. "That sounds terrible. Do you think they'll experiment on us?"

Watch nodded. "It's a possibility. We have to mentally prepare ourselves to have our organs removed, maybe without anesthesia."

"If they remove many of our organs, we'll die."

"It might be a blessing."

Adam stepped back from the transparent wall and sat down on one of the beds. He was exhausted. The time he had spent unconscious from the ray gun zap had not qualified as a refreshing nap. He was also deathly thirsty and hungry. He wondered what the meals would be like.

"You're depressing me," Adam muttered.

"I'm sorry." Watch sat on the bed across from him. "Maybe it's not as hopeless as it appears. We've been in some nasty fixes before, and we've always gotten out. Why should this time be any different?"

"Because this time we're trapped in a cage billions of miles from Earth?"

Watch yawned and leaned back on his bed. "Now you're depressing me."

There was nothing else to say, for the time being.

They both lay down and rested. They may have even dozed.

Time went by. They weren't sure how much.

Without warning they heard a soft knock at the door.

"Hey. Are you in there?"

As Sally predicted, there were four guards waiting for them when they docked. Sally had Ek invite them in so she and Cindy could stun them. They stored the guards belowdecks with the others. To Sally and Cindy's immense relief, no other guards rushed to the scene. Perhaps Ek was partially right—his people were not experts when it came to security. Sally, Cindy, and Ek had time to work.

Unfortunately, Ek was making little progress with his plan. They had been in space dock an hour and he still hadn't been able to locate Adam and

Watch. He was searching through some kind of computer map that was projected on a three-dimensional computer screen located to the left of the saucer control panel. He said it was supposed to register all living creatures on the station.

"I do not understand why they do not show up."

"It's the way I told you," Sally said as she paced behind Ek. "There must be restricted areas aboard this station. You have to forget about trying to find them. Just broadcast on your telepathic network what has happened. Maybe one of the thousands of fatheads—I mean, maybe one of your many network partners—will have an idea where they are."

"I don't know if that's a good idea," Cindy said. "The moment Ek makes such a broadcast, more guards will show up."

Sally was agitated. "I know that. I'm not stupid. But they're going to come here anyway. At least we will have got our message out. Once they arrest us, there'll be no chance. We'll probably be put to immediate death."

"Our culture does not have the death penalty."

"You don't know what your culture does behind

closed doors," Sally snapped. Then she paused, thinking. "How can we protect ourselves inside this ship? When they do come for us?"

"We can lock the door. But they will burn through it quickly, if they want to."

"Can you fire the ship's weapons while we're in space dock?" Sally asked.

"That would not be a good idea. Many could be hurt."

Sally rolled her eyes. "Like I'm worried about a few casualties. Listen, Ek, I am not a violent person by nature but you guys started this, and I intend to finish it. When your authorities show up, we need something to fight them with until we can get Adam and Watch back. Better yet, we need something to *force* them to give us back our friends. Even if we just use it as a bluff."

"What is a bluff?"

"It's what you do when you want to win at poker," Sally said. She pointed to the floor beneath them. "This ship accelerated to near light speed in two hours. It must have a powerful engine or warp drive. What's its source of energy?"

"Our space drive is powered by the decay of an element called Zelithium 110. It cannot be found on

your periodic table of elements because it does not exist naturally, except in the corona of extremely hot blue stars. As the element decays in a chamber of Hyperzoid Quartz, it radiates subatomic particles we call Bostonians. They are very powerful but unstable, unless carefully controlled."

Sally glanced at Cindy. "I got less than half that," Cindy said.

"You say the Bostonians are unstable?" Sally said. "I like things that way. Instability brings out my finer points. Tell me, Ek, can this stuff be used to make a bomb?"

Ek looked as worried as an expressionless alien could.

"Yes. The Hyperzoid Quartz can be tampered with so that the decay of Bostonians builds toward a critical mass."

"What happens when critical mass is reached?" Sally asked.

"There is a huge explosion."

"Would the explosion be strong enough to destroy this space station?" Sally asked.

Ek hesitated. *"Yes. And many stations and vessels in the immediate vicinity."*

"Can you control the decay of the Bostonians so

that we don't accidentally blow ourselves up?" Sally asked.

"Yes. But not well."

"Can you stop the chain reaction once it has begun?"

"Yes. If I am lucky."

"If you start such a chain reaction, will the authorities outside know what you're up to?" Sally asked. "Will they be able to monitor it?"

"Yes."

"Will it scare them?"

The alien lowered his big head.

"Yes. Very much. You could kill millions of my people."

Sally smiled at his sad thought. "Ek, I don't want to kill anybody. I just want to scare your people into giving us back Adam and Watch. But when it comes time to bargain, I have to give the impression that I'm a crazy chick from Spooksville who would just as soon blow up this space station as go swimming in our reservoir at home."

"What is Spooksville?"

"That's where we come from," Sally explained. "And you and your pals are only one of the reasons it has earned that name. You're not even the worst reason. Now broadcast your telepathic message about Adam and Watch and get your Boston bomb ready. Work as fast as you can. I'm still hoping to make it home in time for bed."

Cindy shook her head doubtfully. "You're playing with fire, Sally."

"You don't understand me, Cindy." Sally rubbed her hands together, excited. "I'm playing to win."

12

Hearing the knock on the door, and the telepathic message, Adam and Watch jumped up from the beds and huddled by the door. They could hear nothing outside.

"Who do you think it is?" Adam asked.

"Either Ekwee12 or another alien," Watch said.

"I know it's either Ekwee12 or another alien. Sally and Cindy haven't become telepathic in the last few hours. The question is, what should we do?"

"If it's someone come to rescue us," Watch said "We'll never forgive ourselves if we don't answe

Adam put his mouth close to the door. "Yeah, we're in here. But who are you?"

The telepathic response was immediate.

"Zhekee191."

Adam and Watch stared at each other. "Their names are kind of corny," Adam said.

"Imagine if there are hundreds of Zhekees," Watch agreed.

Adam spoke to the door again. "What do you want?" he asked.

"Are you Adam and Watch? The two human beings?"

"Yes," Adam said. "How did you learn our names?" None of the other aliens, with the exception of Ekwee12, had asked them.

"Ekwee12 came on our youth network and explained that you two had been taken captive by our government, in violation of our laws. He wanted all of us to fan out and search for you. I know Ekwee12 personally. I am his friend and respect what he says. I know he would not joke about such a serious matter."

"How were you able to get into this place?"

"My father works here. I have known for many years that we are not encouraged to visit here and it made me wonder if perhaps this was where you had

been taken captive. I am pleased to find you so quickly. I have my father's passkey. It allows me to enter and exit this section."

"Can you open this door?" Adam asked.

"Yes. I just have to push the button beside the door and it will open."

Again Adam and Watch stared at each other. "He might have said so at the beginning," Adam said.

"Perhaps he's afraid how ugly we'll look," Watch said.

"I know what you look like, of course. I will open the door."

The door opened right then. Zhekee191 could have been Ekwee12's identical twin brother. He stared up at them with his big black almond-shaped eyes.

"You are tall."

"We get taller, as time goes on," Adam said. "Where is Ekwee12?"

"He did not say specifically but he must still be in space dock."

"Do you know if he has our friends Sally and Cindy with him?" Watch asked.

"No. He did not mention them in his message. Are they female humans?"

"Yes." Adam paused. "How did you guess that?"

"I have studied your culture. It is a required class in our schools."

"I didn't know we were so important," Adam said. "Are you guys planning to invade our planet?"

Zhekee191 seemed taken aback.

"We could not do that. It would not be possible."

"Then how or why do you know so much about us?" Watch asked.

"Because you made us who we are. Of course."

"Of course," Adam muttered. He had no idea what the alien was talking about, nor did he really care. He just wanted to get home. He was starving for a real Earth dinner. "Can you take us to space dock?" he asked.

"That is what I wish to do. But we have to be careful. You are not easy to hide. I know a special way there that few take."

"Can you get us a weapon?" Watch asked.

"What do you need a weapon for?"

"Protection," Adam said. "We've already been shot by your people once today. We won't shoot anybody unless we're attacked. You have our word."

"I cannot get you a weapon. I do not even know where they are stored."

"Take us to the space dock then," Adam said. "And thanks ahead of time for all your help."

Watch glanced back in the direction of the captured Hyeet. "I hate to leave that hairy guy. I feel like he's almost one of us."

Adam nodded. "Maybe we can rescue him later. But right now we have to take care of ourselves."

They hurried out of the cell and raced down a long hallway. Right away Adam could see they were going in a different direction from before. The hallways were all similar, but there were also differences. For example, for several hundred yards, they entered a glass hallway that looked out over a massive park area. The green area had to be a mile across. It was crowded with thousands of aliens. Some seemed to be playing games, others were just relaxing by small lakes.

Yet there was no sun in the sky. There was no real sky, actually, just a wide curving ceiling that glowed with gentle yellow light. Adam wondered if Watch might have been right. Maybe the aliens had polluted their planet so badly that they had to live in space, whether they wanted to or not.

Maybe that was why they kept coming to Earth.

To take it over. Adam didn't care what Zhekee191 said.

He was still worried about an invasion.

Adam was glad no one noticed them while they were in the glass hallway.

It would have been hard to outrun thousands.

Yet, before they reached the space dock, they did run into a guard. He appeared to be searching for them. He carried a ray gun and when he saw them he immediately aimed it at them. They received a strong and clear telepathic message at the same time.

"Stop where you are and put your hands over your heads."

Where they were, fortunately, was two feet from a corner. Adam and Watch exchanged quick knowing glances. No way they were going back in that cage. They jumped for cover, behind the corner. There was a flash of green light but it bounced harmlessly off the wall behind them.

Zhekee191 seemed taken by surprise. He remained frozen where they had been spotted by the guard. Watch started to run away, but Adam grabbed his arm and pulled him tight against the wall, right next to the corner.

"Let's take the guard," Adam whispered.

The alien security guard had obviously not grown up on spy movies. The guy came running around the corner without any thought that they might be waiting for him. Adam simply stuck out his foot. The guy tripped; he went down hard. In fact, he seemed to knock himself out when he hit the floor with his big fat head. Adam reached down and grabbed his weapon, which had bounced free. Zhekee191 stared at them with a mixture of wonder and terror.

"You are an interesting species."

"We have our good points," Adam admitted. He showed Zhekee191 the weapon. "How do I control the power on this thing?"

It was very simple. If he turned the little knob clockwise, the power became stronger. There were ten settings. *One* stood for light stun. *Two* was hard stun. *Four* and up could kill, Zhekee191 warned. Adam left the weapon on *two,* where it had originally been set, but he didn't rule out the possibility of increasing the power. They were taking a space ship to Earth, he vowed, one way or the other. Zhekee191 was more worried than ever.

"Please do not hurt anyone."

"We only want to go home," Adam said.

Zhekee191 led them on their way. Ten minutes later they reached the space dock. There was no transition. They were in a narrow hallway one second, then they were in the gigantic space harbor the next. Adam and Watch were stunned to see a crowd of aliens gathered around one saucer. The ship floated at the end of a narrow dock. The aliens were bunched up on the dock like sardines in a can. They had several portable instruments with them, and seemed to be measuring what was going on inside the ship. The vessel looked exactly like the craft they had taken from Earth to the alien station. But Adam quickly realized that this was the one that Sally, Cindy, and Ekwee12 flew.

Adam could dimly sense the buzzing thoughts of the crowd.

The aliens were worried.

And Adam planned to give them one more thing to worry about. He turned the power on his hand weapon up to *ten* and pointed it at the crowd. He had only been taught the rules of poker a few hours earlier but he had learned them well.

"This gun is set to kill!" he shouted. "Stand aside or I'll fire!"

13

After Ek had broadcast his telepathic network message to search for the humans, he started the Zelithium 110–Hyperzoid-Quartz-Bostonian chain reaction. The building critical mass was definitely something the alien scientists could sense with their instruments—if the size of the crowd outside was any indication. Sally had already issued her demand for the release of Adam and Watch. She threatened to blow up the space station if they were not. But so far her friends hadn't been handed over. Sally believed that the chain reaction would have to get closer to the critical point before the aliens would do what she wanted.

But it was getting there quick.

At what Ek called Level 84 Bostonian the reactor would blow.

They were now at Level 65.

Ek did not believe he could stop the reaction after Level 80.

"We're lucky they haven't tried to burn down the door," Cindy muttered, watching the viewing ports along the wall.

Ek looked up from the control panel.

"They are afraid we will speed up the reaction if they try."

Sally continued to pace. The tension was growing unbearable.

"We're not leaving without them," Sally muttered.

"I don't get you," Cindy said. "One minute you were ready to fly home without them. The next you're ready to sacrifice millions of lives to get to them."

"A girl has a right to change her mind," Sally said.

"Are your people willing to sacrifice this station

to prevent Adam and Watch from escaping?" Cindy asked Ek, feeling desperate.

"I would have said no. My people cherish life. I do not understand why they are being so stubborn." Ek glanced at his instruments. *"We have jumped to Level 72."*

"So quickly?" Cindy asked, shocked.

"The reaction accelerates as it reaches critical mass."

"How much time do we have?" Sally asked.

"To stop the reaction, maybe three of your minutes. To the explosion, five minutes."

"We have to back down," Cindy said.

"We're not backing down!" Sally said. "A bluff doesn't work unless you push it to the limit!"

"At the reservoir you were bluffing with rocks!" Cindy said. "That was not gambling. *This* is gambling. You're risking our lives."

"No guts, no glory," Sally said. Yet she seemed uncertain. She paused in midstride, thoughtful. "Ek, you haven't recently checked your computer map of where everyone is supposed to be. Try locating Adam and Watch now."

"What are you thinking?" Cindy asked.

"Maybe the aliens don't know where Adam and Watch are. So they can't hand them over to us."

"That's impossible," Cindy said.

"Not if they've escaped," Sally said.

Once again Ek failed to locate Adam and Watch on his computer map. But it didn't matter. Glancing again out the viewing ports right then, Cindy almost had a heart attack.

"There they are!" Cindy screamed. "It's Adam and Watch!"

Sally pounded her fist in the air. "I knew the bluff would work!"

"No!" Cindy said quickly. "The aliens are not handing them over willingly. Adam has a gun. He's pointing it at the crowd. They must have broken free."

"Just as I suspected," Sally said. She turned to Ek. "Open hailing frequencies."

"What?"

"She wants to talk to the outside," Cindy explained. "Is there a way?"

"Yes. Of course." Ek pushed a button. *"Speak and they will hear you."*

"How close are we now?" Sally asked Ek.

"Level 75. We have less than two minutes to stop the chain reaction."

Sally cleared her throat and spoke loudly and formally. "Adam, Watch—this is Captain Sara

Wilcox of the *Starship UFO*. I am pleased to see you've escaped, and I approve of your resorting to blatant force to fight your way to freedom. But I feel an obligation to inform you that my starship is going to explode in two minutes and that everything for a radius of one thousand miles will be completely destroyed. Over?"

Outside, near the dock, Adam and Watch looked at each other. "I think the power has gone to her brain," Watch said.

"Is she bluffing?" Adam asked.

"I hope so," Watch said. He gestured to the crowd of aliens that separated them from the ship. "I think she's trying to scare these guys into letting all of us go."

Zhekee191 shifted uneasily beside them.

"She is scaring me. I would be happy to let you go."

Adam sighed, the gun still in his hand. "I don't know what to do. I can't really fire this thing. I might hurt somebody."

"Somebody has to back down," Watch said darkly. "Or soon none of us will be feeling any pain."

Inside the ship Ek informed Sally that they had jumped to Level 78.

"We have less than a minute."

"Why don't they let us go?" Sally demanded, getting exasperated. "Can't they see that I'm serious? Do they want to die?"

"I do not understand them. I do not understand why they kidnapped you in the first place."

"We must stop the chain reaction!" Cindy cried. "The bluff has failed!"

"We can't stop!" Sally shouted back. "If we do we'll never get out of here!"

"We have jumped to Level 79."

"I would rather be alive here than dead!" Cindy yelled.

"How do you know they'd let us live?" Sally demanded.

"I say we stop it!" Cindy shouted. "And I have as much say as you! Ek, pull the plug!"

"Which plug am I supposed to pull?"

"Wait!" Sally cried.

"Wait for what?" Cindy screamed. "Death?"

"Do it then!" Sally shouted bitterly, turning away. "Surrender. That's all you're good for."

Cindy bent over the control panel beside Ek. "Stop the reaction. Do it now."

Ek's four-fingered hands flew over the control panel. Then he sat perfectly still, waiting for some reaction to the chain reaction. He raised his big head to look at Cindy. His whole body seemed to twitch.

"It is too late."

"What?" Cindy whispered.

"We have jumped to Level 81. Nothing can stop it from exploding."

Cindy felt the life go out of her. She glanced over at Sally.

"Well, you got what you wanted," Cindy said to her back. "We're doomed."

Sally seemed to freeze for a second, then suddenly she whirled on Ek. "Can we fly the ship out of space dock?" she asked. "If we tell them we can't stop it, and they let us go, do we have time to get the ship clear of the station?"

Ek consulted his instruments.

"Yes. I can still maneuver the ship. If they let us go, we can move it out of the station before the explosion."

"Talk to them," Sally said. "Send a strong thought, whatever. Hurry!" Sally stepped to Cindy and put a hand on her shoulder. "You get off the ship. I'll ride out with Ek. I got him in this mess. If he has to die, I'll die with him."

Cindy patted her hand. "Sally, you amaze me. You're so brave."

Ek jumped up quickly.

"They have opened the outside station doors for us. I have programmed the ship to fly into deep space. None of us has to stay here. None of us has to die."

"Actually," Sally admitted with a faint smile, "I was hoping he was going to say that."

They released the six guards belowdecks, and the nine of them jumped outside onto the dock. They were hardly clear of the ship when it took off at high speed behind them. They caught a flash of it disappearing through the huge dark entrance, then it was gone. A minute went by while aliens and humans alike held their breaths. Sally and Cindy waited for a huge shock wave, but none came. All at once a wave of relief seemed to move through the gathering. Ek calmly informed them that the ship had exploded safely out of the way.

"But we didn't feel anything?" Sally said. "Was it a huge explosion?"

"Yes. But the ship is fast. It took place far from here, and there is no shock wave in space. You would not feel anything unless we were being destroyed."

Sally nodded wearily. "Well, it's done then. We're caught."

The crowd parted so that the four humans could be together. Adam surrendered his gun. There seemed no point in keeping it after a nuclear bomb had failed to move the aliens to release them. The guys patted the girls on their backs.

"Thank you for coming for us," Adam said.

"That was an awesome bluff," Watch agreed. "I would have fallen for it."

Sally shook her head. "Not you. You're too cool a player."

Watch glanced at Adam. "I'm not saying anything," Adam said.

There was nothing to say. Alien guards grabbed hold of their arms. The crude message was clear. They were going to be taken to the cages. Ekwee12 and Zhekee191 tried to protest, but they were pulled aside by government authorities. Adam wondered what their punishment would be. He felt almost as bad for them as he did for himself and his friends. And they had come so close to escaping. It made the final defeat that much more bitter.

Yet all was not lost.

All around the circular space port, on maybe fifty different levels, young aliens poured into view.

There were dozens at first, then hundreds. Within a couple of minutes, as Adam and his friends stood spellbound, the number swelled to at least two thousand. None of the aliens was over two feet tall, but their combined telepathic message was clear, and very powerful.

"LET THE HUMANS GO! THEY HAVE DONE US NO HARM!"

Ek broke free of the authorities and hurried to their side.

His thoughts were excited.

"These are my friends on the network. They are not going to let this injustice continue. They are demanding your release."

Adam laughed. "Even we dull humans are able to pick up that kind of mental message. The question is, will your authorities do what your kids say?"

"I think they will have to. In our culture, kids are allowed to vote."

"Cool," Sally said. "If that was true in our culture, I would be president."

Another few minutes went by. The alien authorities huddled. The alien guards continued to hold on to the humans. But as time passed, more kids flooded the area. The huddled aliens seemed to grow even more uneasy. The young aliens' mental voice was like a huge washing wave of reason that could not be ignored. Finally a tall alien dressed in a gold suit took Ekwee12 aside. They conferred for a minute or two, then Ekwee12 literally ran to their side. He took Adam's and Sally's hands and looked up at them with his big black eyes. Once again, he tried to smile. It was a good effort; this time there was real joy in the expression.

"They are letting you go. They have told me to take you home."

Far out in space, almost to the hyperjump, Sally said that Cindy had said that Adam looked like Ekwee12. Adam was taken aback by the remark; he felt insulted.

"I don't believe Cindy said any such thing," Adam replied.

"She did," Sally insisted. "Just ask her."

Adam looked at Cindy. "Well?"

Cindy hesitated. "I said Ek *reminded* me of you. I didn't say you looked alike."

"How do I remind you of an alien?" Adam wanted to know.

Ek spoke from his place at the control panel.

"We are both cute."

"That's it, exactly," Cindy said with a smile.

Adam had to laugh. "I suppose I've been called worse."

"It makes me sick that he is flattered even by her insults," Sally said to Watch.

"You're the captain," Watch said. "Why don't you have them both thrown overboard?" Before leaving, the aliens had given him his watches back, so he was happy. Actually, both of them had gotten their clothes back.

"I've already gone to too much trouble to save them," Sally muttered.

Ek turned and looked at them.

"We are almost to the jump. I was wondering what precise time you would like to be returned?"

That made them all sit up.

"Can this ship travel in time?" Watch asked.

"Of course. You traveled in time on the journey here. Did you not know that?"

"How could we know?" Adam said. "We thought this was just a regular spaceship."

"But you saw how much Earth had changed. You must have known we had jumped forward in time."

They all stared at one another, shocked.

"Do you mean that you are from Earth?" Adam

asked, barely able to get the words out. "In the future?"

"Yes. I thought you knew."

Sally was disgusted. "But you're a fatheaded . . . I mean, you're such an unusual alien shape. I don't understand."

"I am not an alien. I told you."

"But where have all the people on Earth gone?" Sally asked. "Did you invade and wipe them all out?"

Ek shook his head. He must have picked up the gesture being with them.

"We are the people of Earth. We are what you will change into after another two hundred thousand years of evolution."

Sally was indignant. "No way. My great-great-great-grandchildren are not going to look like you. I won't have it."

"I think you need another two thousand *greats* in front of *grandchildren* to match the time frame he's talking about," Watch said.

"If we do become you," Adam said. "Why do you live in space?"

Ek lowered his head.

"You, we—we dirtied our planet. We cannot live there anymore."

"But now that we know that," Adam said hopefully, "maybe we can work in our lives to stop people from polluting the Earth so much. I know I'll try, as soon as I grow up and get out of Spooksville and get a real life."

Ek raised his head. Once more he tried to smile. *"That could help us all."*

"I don't know if I accept this," Sally said. "But for the sake of argument, say you are a more advanced form of us. Why would your people go into the past to steal us? For what purpose?"

"I meant to tell you this. When I conferred with our highest government official, he apologized and said that the government had wanted a few kids from your generation to study to see how to liven up our culture. Lately we have become somewhat stagnant as a race."

Sally laughed. "He got more than he bargained for."

"That is precisely what he conveyed to me. He thought we needed kids from an earlier, calmer generation. You guys were too explosive. But in either case, he promised that anyone else we took from the past would not be kidnapped. They would come with us only if they wanted to come."

"Can you see about getting that Hyeet freed?"

Watch said. "He was in the cage across from us. He looked pretty miserable."

"Now that we know the truth, the youth of our culture will demand that no intelligent creature be kept hostage. It should not have happened to begin with."

"I agree with that," Cindy said. "This has been a long day."

"That is what I'm asking you. I can return you home to any time you wish. You only have to tell me when."

"We should probably return just after we were kidnapped," Adam suggested. "After both ships left. I don't want to go running into myself."

"I agree," Watch said.

"Sounds good," Sally said. "That way we can make it home in time for dinner."

But Cindy suddenly jumped up. "We have to land before we left. We have to come in unobserved, and land on the hill near the Haunted Cave."

"Why?" they all asked.

Cindy was thoughtful. "It's hard to explain. Just trust me on this one. Ek, do you have a ray gun aboard this ship?"

"Yes. Why?"

"I will need to borrow it just after we land. Put us

down right before the two ships appeared. But like I said, don't let anyone—including ourselves—see us."

"Cindy," Adam warned. "We don't want to tamper with time. Let our earlier versions go have the adventure. It was fun, and it turned out all right in the end."

But Cindy was adamant. "No. This way is the only way. You'll see why when we get there."

Since Cindy refused to change her mind, they instructed Ek to do what she said. Ek adjusted the hyperjump so that they burst through to their time a few hours early. In fact, it gave them enough leeway so they were able to swing by Jupiter, Saturn, and Mars for a look. Watch said the planets were much more impressive up close than in his telescope.

"I'm going to have to get one of these saucers," he said with a sigh.

Finally they landed on the hill near the Haunted Cave. Ek had turned off the saucer's lights. They came down unobserved and slipped out of the ship. It was still warm but good to be back and feel normal dirt beneath their feet. Even if they were back in Spooksville, home was home.

Far below, they could see themselves, sitting by the reservoir.

The earlier Cindy was still soaking her foot in the water.

"Oh," Cindy now said, wincing as she put her foot down. "You guys have to help me down the ravine. Ek, I need that gun."

"Are you injured, Cindy?"

"Yes. I sprained my ankle before you showed up."

"Why didn't you tell me? I have something that will fix that."

Ek disappeared inside. When he returned he had a ray gun and a small silver ball. Instructing Cindy to sit down, he placed it near her ankle. The ball began to glow a dull red color. After a couple of minutes Cindy let out a soft cry of delight. She flexed her foot and Ek withdrew the strange instrument.

"My ankle's all better! How did you do that, Ek?"

"We know a lot more about human, and alien, bodies in our time."

"Great." Cindy jumped up and grabbed the weapon. "I have a job I have to take care of. The first setting is stun, right Ek?"

"That is correct."

"Who are you going to stun?" Adam insisted.

"You'll see," Cindy said. "You guys can come with me if you're real quiet."

Together, Ek included, they crept down the hill, until they were almost able to hear the earlier versions of themselves talking. No surprise, two alien ships suddenly appeared in the sky. They watched everything that had happened before, up until Watch was taken inside the first saucer. Then Cindy said they had to move closer.

"We shouldn't interfere," Sally repeated.

"We won't," Cindy promised. "Everything will be just as it was."

They crept cautiously around until they were at the lip of ravine. Down below, the fighting started. Adam and Sally were stunned by the alien weapons. But back up on the hill, to everyone's surprise—except Cindy's—two aliens walked by just below them. To their even greater surprise, they saw an earlier version of Cindy stand up on the opposite side of the ravine. She had a big rock in her hands.

Her intention was clear. She was going to brain one or both of the aliens. They watched in amazement as she raised the rock above her head and threw it down. At that exact instant, *their* Cindy whipped out her gun and aimed and fired. There was a flash of green light. She stunned the aliens, and the two collapsed in a pile. The rock had missed by a mile. Cindy laughed quietly beside them in the dark as her earlier version peered confused over the edge of the ravine.

"I wondered why those guys just fell over on me," she whispered.

Epilogue

It was time to say goodbye to Ekwee12. They hated to see him leave.

"Why don't you hang out with us for awhile?" Adam asked. "There's always a lot happening here. Things are never 'stagnant.' "

"Yeah, you can learn a lot from us about how awesome kids in this century are," Sally said.

"I would love to stay. But I have work to do at home cleaning up the confusion caused by your illegal capture. I have to return and make sure it never happens again."

"But when you're done with your job, stop by

some time," Cindy pleaded. "We like you. You're one of us."

Ekwee12 held out his hands for each of them to touch.

"You will see me again. I promise."

They said their goodbyes. Cindy had a tear in her eye. Maybe they all did. But just as Ekwee12 was about to disappear inside his ship, Sally called out one last question.

"Hey, Ek?" she said. "Do you know why it's so hot here these days? We never have weather like this."

"A heavy inversion layer has settled over this portion of your coast. It will clear up in a couple of days and then you will have cooler temperatures."

"It's not a witch's curse, after all," Adam teased her.

Sally nodded, insulted. "I knew that."

About the Author

Little is known about Christopher Pike, although he is supposed to be a strange man. It is rumored that he was born in New York but grew up in Los Angeles. He has been seen in Santa Barbara lately, so he probably lives there now. But no one really knows what he looks like, or how old he is. It is possible that he is not a real person, but an eccentric creature visiting from another world. When he is not writing, he sits and stares at the walls of his huge haunted house. A short, ugly troll wanders around him in the dark and whispers scary stories in his ear.

Christopher Pike is one of this planet's best-selling authors of young adult fiction.